THIS LITTLE PIRATE

THIS Little

Pirate

by PHILEMON STURGES

illustrated by AMY WALROD

DUTTON CHILDREN'S BOOKS ★ NEW YORK

To Donna Brooks, an amazing editor who taught me how
to make hens cluck, dogs sniff, and pigs celebrate!
—P.S.

For Little Lucas, with love.
And special thanks to Amiko, who kept me smiling
and laughing on my desert island.
—A.W.

DUTTON CHILDREN'S BOOKS A division of Penguin Young Readers Group
Published by the Penguin Group · Penguin Group (USA) Inc, 375 Hudson Street, New York, New York 10014, U.S.A.
Penguin Group (Canada), 10 Alcorn Avenue, Toronto, Ontario, Canada M4V 3B2 (a division of Pearson Penguin Canada Inc.) ·
Penguin Books Ltd, 80 Strand, London WC2R 0RL, England · Penguin Ireland, 25 St Stephen's Green, Dublin 2, Ireland (a divi-
sion of Penguin Books Ltd) · Penguin Group (Australia), 250 Camberwell Road, Camberwell, Victoria 3124, Australia (a division
of Pearson Australia Group Pty Ltd) · Penguin Books India Pvt Ltd, 11 Community Centre, Panchsheel Park, New Delhi - 110
017, India · Penguin Group (NZ), Cnr Airborne and Rosedale Roads, Albany, Auckland 1310, New Zealand (a division of Pearson
New Zealand Ltd) · Penguin Books (South Africa) (Pty) Ltd, 24 Sturdee Avenue, Rosebank, Johannesburg 2196, South Africa ·
Penguin Books Ltd, Registered Offices: 80 Strand, London WC2R 0RL, England

Library of Congress Cataloging-in-Publication Data
Sturges, Philemon.
  This little pirate/by Philemon Sturges; illustrated by Amy Walrod.—1st ed.
    p. cm.
  Summary: Two bands of pirates fight over a box, but when they raise
the white flag and open the box together, they find a treasure to share.
  ISBN 0-525-46440-9 (alk. paper)
  [1. Pirates—Fiction. 2. Buried treasure—Fiction. 3. Parties—Fiction.
4. Pigs—Fiction 5. Stories in rhyme] I. Walrod, Amy, ill II. Title.
  PZ8.3.S9227Th 2005
  [E]—dc22 2004020907

Published in the United States by Dutton Children's Books,
a division of Penguin Young Readers Group
345 Hudson Street, New York, New York 10014
www.penguin.com/youngreaders
Designed by Irene Vandervoort
Manufactured in China   First Edition
10 9 8 7 6 5 4 3 2 1

This little pirate
spied the island.

This little pirate
saw the rocks.

This little pirate
dropped the anchor,

and this little pirate
found the box.

Then this big pirate yelled, "Yo-ho-ho!
The box is ours and home we'll go!"

This little pirate
rowed the rowboat.

This little
pirate shouted,
"Rocks!"

This little pirate
made the landing,

and this little pirate hollered, "Box!"

Then this big pirate yelled, "Yo-ho-ho!
This box is *ours*, and home *you'll* go!"

So this little pirate
threw a tantrum,

and this frightened
pirate cried, "Duck!"

Then this spunky pirate
showed her muscle,

and this nasty pirate
said, "Yuck!"

When this angry pirate smashed a seashell,

this grouchy pirate kicked a pail.

When this silly pirate made a mad face,

this naughty pirate pulled her tail.

Then those ten rowdy pirates
wrestled and whooped

till they were all *completely*...

pooped!

Then this big pirate waved a white truce flag,
and this big pirate did, too.
"Why don't we try to open the top?"
asked the exasperated crew.

So four little pirates found a rope,

and four more climbed a tree.

Then the two big pirates tied a secret knot,

and they all pulled—one, two, THREE!

The top popped off, and they looked inside.
"It's party stuff!" those pirates cried.

So these little pirates baked a great big cake,

and these little pirates made spoons.

These clever pirates made enormous hats,

and these puffing pirates filled balloons.

Those ten hungry pirates all ate like pigs—
They burp-slurp-gobble-guzzled fast.
Then they grabbed their presents—
"OH, WOW!" they roared.
"Let's have a mighty pirate BLAST!"

So this little pirate blew his trumpet,

and this one banged her drum.

This mellow pirate played his saxophone,

and this one hummed a hum.

The two big pirates just jigged all about
till the sun went down and the stars came out.

When the red crab ate the last cookie
and the fat clam polished off the cake,
the eight little pirates discovered
that they just couldn't stay awake.

So these tired pirates
rowed to the boats

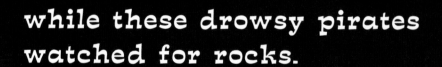

while these drowsy pirates
watched for rocks.

As these sleepy pirates
set the towline,

these groggy pirates stowed the box.

Then these weary
pirates put on
jammies.

These worn-out
pirates said,
" 'Night."

As these tuckered
pirates hugged
teddies,

these pooped pirates slept tight.

But the two big pirates stayed up till dawn
with nary a nod and not one yawn.
And they sang as they sailed 'neath the starry dome,
"Yo-ho-ho!
Ho-ho-ho!"

All the way home!